The Olive Tree

By Georgene Freedman

Illustrations by Joan Keefer-Bowden

Simpatico Books™

Special mention for our pet dove named "Lovey" that came to us through an open balcony window and stayed with us for 8 years...*never was there a more gentle creature.*

$\mathfrak{T}$his story began over 2,000 years ago in a far away city called Jerusalem. . .

There once was an ordinary turtle dove named Esther who had a pretty extraordinary problem. Doves are always found in pairs, but Esther never found another dove to share her life with. She had always dreamed of having a baby dove, but was starting to fear that she might never have an egg to call her own.

Every spring she would work so hard to build a most magnificent nest, but by summers end the nest would still be empty. This made Esther very sad. Thinking that a change of scenery would do her good, she decided to leave her home and look for a new place to live.

Esther flew and flew until she came upon the most charming garden she could have ever imagined. This garden was called "Gethsemane" and she decided instantly that she would make this garden her home for the rest of her life.

$\mathfrak{W}$hile searching for the ideal tree in which to make
her new home, Esther noticed the most heavenly nest
perched in a majestic olive tree – the oldest tree in the
garden. She spied it from afar at first, but could not resist
taking a closer look. To her amazement there was an egg
in the nest   the most beautiful egg she had ever seen.
Oh, how she wished this egg could be hers.

She guarded the nest from branches above for the rest of the day and all through the night. Its owner had not returned in all that time to care for the egg. Esther waited, never leaving the olive tree; not even to eat.

She watched over the nest…until another day had passed. Concerned, she decided that whoever owned this nest surely must have had a very good reason for not returning to such a perfect egg.

An egg needs to be kept warm to survive; a mother bird would never leave her egg for so long. Esther flew down to the nest and as she got closer noticed a golden glow surrounding the egg. When she reached the nest she gently sat upon the egg. Never was there a more devoted dove in the garden. Her love for the little abandoned egg grew until her heart could hold no more love.

Then, one very peaceful morning in late spring, the egg began to move! It rocked, and it shook, and suddenly tiny cracks began to appear. Out poked the head of the most enchanting baby dove, the only pure white dove ever to inhabit the garden.

"Mama!" the hatchling exclaimed.

This *chosen* mother could hardly believe her eyes! Esther named the baby 'Lovey.'

𝕿his garden had been blessed….it was the most tranquil
place in the whole world. Esther nurtured her gift from
God. She fed Lovey and taught her to fly, but most of
all she *loved* her, as only a mother can love. It wasn't long
before Esther realized that Lovey also had a special gift
from God – she had one of the most peaceful coos ever
to be heard in the garden. Never, since the beginning of
time was there a dove with such a peaceful coo. All coos
are soothing, but Lovey's coo was extra special.

Lovey and her mother spent many hours just gazing
into each others eyes   envisioning all the wonderful days
that lay ahead of them in their Garden of Gethsemane.
Their days consisted of flying from one delicious tree
to another eating the endless supply of fruits and seeds.
Their favorite times were spent playing and bathing in a
nearby brook. At nightfall they would cuddle and sleep
in their special olive tree, the most revered tree in all the
garden.

On awakening one cloudy and dreary morning, Lovey
noticed that her mother was not there. Esther sometimes
liked to wake up early and gather breakfast, but something
was very wrong in the garden this morning. Then, Lovey
heard those strange noises that often made birds fly high
up into the trees. Esther had taught Lovey to stay away
from humans, but Lovey went to investigate the noise
anyway. She heard rustling and swooshing sounds, and
then she could hear the frantic calls of her mother! Poor
Esther had been caught in a net and placed in a basket by
a man. Lovey flew at once to help her mother, but Esther
ordered her to return to the safety of their olive tree
and to never look back again!

Lovey disobeyed her mother and followed the man who had captured Esther all the way to a big house set high on a hilltop. Hundreds of people were entering this place called 'temple' to study and pray   and to offer gifts to God. Some people were bringing lambs into the temple with them   while others brought doves into this big house of God.

Lovey hid in a nearby tree hoping that her mother would return. She noticed that all the lambs and doves that entered the temple were not coming back out. Only the humans that had brought the animals in were coming back out – and they were coming out without the animals. After a very long time Lovey sadly returned to the olive tree in the garden.

While it was the first time in her young life that Lovey was ever alone and although she was very scared, she stayed in the olive tree she was born in – hardly ever leaving it. She felt safe and peaceful tucked within its branches. She could barely eat of the same trees or drink from the same brook she once so happily shared with her mother, Esther. More worrisome was that Lovey hadn't cooed since the loss of her mother. A dove that doesn't coo is a very, very unhappy dove. The garden would never be the same.

Then, one moonlit night a stillness and hush fell over the garden. Suddenly, Lovey felt a warm breeze and heard a soft voice rustling through the leaves of the old olive tree. The voice was familiar to her and seemed to be calling her name ever so softly…

"Lovey"….."Lovey"…it called out to her. Lovey perked up quickly, for she knew it was the voice of her mother! She could see Esther in a warm golden glow of light.

"Mother, oh mother you've come back!" exclaimed Lovey.

"Yes, I'm here my darling," answered Esther.

"Where have you been mother? You look so beautiful!" exclaimed Lovey.

"Oh Lovey, I am in the most heavenly place, even more beautiful than our Garden of Gethsemane, "she answered. "It's a glorious place…I now live in God's special garden in heaven called Paradise."

"I want to be with you mother. Please take me with you. I've missed you so much," cried Lovey.

"I cannot take you with me just yet Lovey – there is a very important purpose in your life that you must fulfill."

" What purpose mother? I'll do anything to be with you!" pleaded Lovey.

"You'll know soon enough my daughter," answered Esther.

"How did you get to paradise Mother?" asked Lovey.

"I was offered as a gift to God at the temple   and because I was an offering to God, my reward is that I will live in Paradise forever!"

Esther explained to Lovey that she would have to stay on earth until she fulfilled her purpose…no matter how long it took. She told how lambs and doves were given as gifts or *offerings* to God at the Temple and how those special animals were permitted to live in paradise. All other animals and humans must earn their way to paradise by always treating others with love, respect and kindness and being godly.

"Some day you will join me here Lovey, but for now I must go," vowed Esther. Lovey begged her mother not to leave her again, but she told Lovey that she must. The last words she heard from Esther were, "Lovey, you must *promise me* that you'll leave the Garden of Gethsemane to find a new home – and you must do this tomorrow. I will always love you." And with that Esther was gone.

"But mother, I don't want to ever leave *our olive tree* and *our* garden….where will I go?" sobbed Lovey.

Lovey fell into a deep sleep and when morning came, it seemed as if it had all been a dream. Lovey knew in her heart that it wasn't a dream, and that she must keep her promise to her mother.

As the sun rose, Lovey flew through the garden and over the brook, while visions of all the wonderful times spent with her mother flashed through her mind.

Then she flew back to their olive tree one last time. This tree would be the hardest of all to leave; she had never been away from it before. Lovey was leaving her garden. The sad old olive tree seemed to embrace her with its branches. The wise old tree knew that Lovey had to leave the garden.

$\mathfrak{L}$ovey wasn't flying for very long when she came upon
a small Judean town called Bethlehem. She was sad and
confused about where she was to go, yet somehow she
was being drawn to this little town. In the distance she
saw a stable that was home to a cow and its calf. There
were shepherds tending to their sheep in grassy meadows,
and it suddenly seemed like a nice place to start anew.
Lovey felt deep inside that she was to make her new
home here....and so she did.

She followed her instincts and built her nest up in the rafters of the humble little stable where cows and sheep slept each night. A few months passed and Lovey had become very fond of her new home and friends. When once upon a star-filled night a man leading a donkey carrying a woman arrived at the stable. Lovey knew immediately that she need not fear *this* man, for his was the face of a kind and gentle man. He made a bed out of straw for the woman he called…Mary.

During this most wondrous night, Lovey and the animals witnessed the miracle of all miracles! The woman Mary gave birth to a baby boy. For the first time in a very long time…Lovey cooed!!! Her cooing soothed Mary and her newborn son named Jesus. For several nights her peaceful cooing lulled this Holy Child in the manger to sleep.

Over the next few days Lovey's cooing greeted many a King and shepherd alike who traveled far with gifts for this holy child. She had *almost* fulfilled her purpose in life. Once this holy family went on their way, Lovey *knew* it was time to return to her olive tree in the Garden of Gethsemane where she was born. So, Lovey flew back to the place she loved most on earth to live out her life in her beloved olive tree. The wise old tree always knew she would be back. The tree welcomed Lovey with open arms!

And 33 years later...the baby Jesus who was born in the stable would come to the Garden of Gethsemane to pray to His Heavenly Father...as He was about to become the gift *'offering'* for all of mankind. Jesus would pray for calm under the wisest olive tree in the garden, and Lovey would be there waiting to soothe Jesus once again with her peaceful cooing.

$\mathfrak{F}$or Lovey was the *dove of peace*! It was her cooing that welcomed the baby Jesus into the world and then calmed Jesus before He left the world. For then was Lovey's purpose finally fulfilled…and was she able to join Esther in paradise forever!

Lovey ✝

Dove of Peace

All of God's children and creatures have a special purpose in life…it can be a small purpose or a grand one…all we have to do is listen carefully to that feeling deep inside of us and follow our hearts to find it.

The author would love for you to visit
www.HeartbeatDesigns.com
and share how you enjoyed "The Olive Tree."
Also let Georgene know if you would like for her
to design a charm in tribute to the story of Lovey!
Your comments could be used on
TheOliveTreeBook.Com web site!